Stolen Pony

Written and Illustrated
by GLEN ROUNDS

Cover illustration by Lydia Rosier

SCHOLASTIC BOOK SERVICES
New York Toronto London Auckland Sydney Tokyo

ISBN: 0-590-32297-4

Copyright 1948, 1969, by Holiday House, Inc. All rights reserved. This edition is published by Scholastic Book Services, a division of Scholastic Inc., 50 West 44th Street, New York, N.Y. 10036, by arrangement with Holiday House, Inc.

12 11 10 9 8 7 6 5 4 3 2 1   11   1 2 3 4 5 6/8

Printed in the U.S.A.   11

Another book by Glen Rounds
available through Scholastic Book Services

The Blind Colt

Horse Thieves

The shaggy ranch dog lay curled up in the grass, and the spotted pony grazed quietly nearby. Over by the corrals the windmill creaked and clanked complainingly in the night wind that blew off the prairie, and one of the saddle horses grazing farther off occasionally stamped or cleared his nostrils. Jack rabbits drifted jerkily back and forth across the flat, looking like odd highbehind shadows in the dusk.

After a time a door slammed up at the ranch house where an old cowpuncher and a boy were getting their supper by the yellow light of a lantern hanging from the kitchen ceiling. The pony threw up his head and held his breath as he listened, and soon he heard footsteps on the path to the corrals. He listened a little longer, then walked carefully over to the sleeping dog. He snuffed softly at the warm furry smell of him,

and nudged him gently with his muzzle. The dog opened one eye and thumped his bushy tail on the ground a couple of times, before he got up to yawn and stretch. He touched noses with the pony then, and trotted over to the gate by the windmill with the pony following close behind.

The boy came up with a little pan of grain and crawled over the gate. He talked to the pony and petted him while the pony nuzzled him over, searching for the grain, and shoved playfully on his chest with his forehead. After a little the boy let the pony eat the grain from his hand, liking the feel of the soft muzzle in his palm. The dog trotted away to inspect the fence corners and the shadows around the ranch buildings on his way to the house where his own supper was waiting by the doorstep. After the pony finished the grain the boy petted him and talked to him for a while longer, and then climbed over the fence and went up to the ranch house.

The pony grazed restlessly close by the fence until the dog came trotting back out of the dark.

He sniffed around the pony's feet and muzzle, tramped out another bed in the grass, and curled up to sleep again with his bushy tail covering his nose and paws like a muff. The spotted pony moved over and stood dozing with his muzzle almost in the sleeping dog's fur.

The grazing horses gradually quieted down and went to sleep. The rabbits were invisible in the full dark, with only an occasional small sneeze or a thumping signal from powerful hind feet to show that they were still busy foraging. The light in the ranch house went out when the boy and the old cowpuncher went to bed. The windmill made the only large noise there was, except for a lone coyote far off, trying to sound like a pack as he yapped from some little hill-top.

Later on in the night a small moon came up over the edge of the prairie and woke the dog. He went off to look around the sleeping ranch, as he was in the habit of doing several times a night. The pony stirred and nickered softly when the dog left, then shifted his weight to the other hip and went back to his doze.

A little later he was wakened by the sound of a truck motor, and in a few minutes a big van running without lights pulled quietly off the road and stopped beside the fence. The pony threw up his head, listening. He heard men get out and stand by the fence, talking in low voices.

After a little, a strange voice said, "That's the one, standin' over there all by his lonesome. Bring a halter and we'll catch him if he's as gentle as I think he is."

The pony heard one of the men rummaging round in the truck for the halter, then the creaking and grunting as they crawled through the barbwire. In a few minutes they had him hemmed up in a fence corner, and the halter put on him. He was frightened at the smells and voices of strange men, and whinnied shrilly for the dog. But the dog was too far away to hear. The men spoke softly to him and handled him gently so he only snorted softly and trembled as they adjusted the straps. Then they led him to the fence where one of the men was already busy with staple pullers taking the wire down.

"Make mighty sure yuh git that wire put

8

back up jest like it was," one voice said after the pony had been led across the lowered wires. "No use advertisin' the fact that we been takin' liberties with this scissorbill's fence."

A cleated ramp was let down from the back of the van and the horse thieves led the pony up the easy slant and inside, where he heard and smelled other horses. They were tied so they stood crosswise of the truck, with loose, slatted stall sections set up between them so they'd not kick or trample each other. The spotted pony was led in and another set of stall slats put in place beside him. After the men had climbed down from the truck the pony heard them putting up the ramp and shutting the doors. The feeling of being closed in the strange place frightened him. Whenever he or one of the other horses shifted weight, the springs creaked and the body of the truck gave and made the footing seem insecure. He stood sweating and shaking, with his feet braced hard while the men talked outside.

"Jest room for one more in there t' make our load," one of the voices said as the horse thieves

moved around to the front of the truck. "Know where we can pick up another one right quick, Joe?"

"There's a bay gelding I got spotted about a mile from here."

"Well, let's go get him!" the first voice said.

Then the motor started and the truck creaked and groaned over the bumps and into the road while the horses inside gathered their feet and braced themselves against the swaying and shifting of the floor. As the truck gathered speed, the spotted pony heard the dog barking outside and whinnied to him. The dog heard and ran behind the truck, yelping, until he was finally left behind.

After the truck had disappeared in the dark, the dog slowed from his frantic running to a pattering trot and kept on in the direction the horse thieves had taken. He had gone a mile or more and was panting hard with his tongue hanging and foam-flecked when he saw the truck loom up in the darkness.

He slowed down and approached it cautiously, his feet making only the smallest sounds in the

deep dust. When he got close he stopped and licked his chops and stuffed his tongue back in his mouth, while he listened carefully. The only sounds were the small crackings and poppings of the truck motor as it cooled, and an occasional noise from one of the horses. He went on and sniffed carefully around the truck until he came to the back, where he found the doors open and the ramp down. The men were gone but he could smell and hear the horses inside.

While he was sniffing around the ramp the pony heard him and whinnied softly. The dog gave an answering whine, scrambled up into the truck, and squeezed under the boards of the pony's stall. They touched noses and sniffed each other and made small pleased noises.

The dog explored the stall and sniffed around the pony's feet. Then, after he'd stuck his nose inquisitively through the slats to smell the horse in the next stall, he sat down against the pony's front legs and panted noisily while he waited for what would happen next.

The other horses had snorted and stamped a little while the dog was scrambling and sniffing around, but when he settled down they soon forgot him, and it was quiet in the van when the horse thieves came back leading another horse. At the first sounds of their return the dog had bristled. When the man with the lead rope stepped up the ramp into the van the dog growled low in his throat. The thief said something in a startled voice and reached in his pants for a flashlight. When he turned it on and saw the dog's eyes glowing in the light, he backed hastily out onto the ramp.

"Watch that light in there!" a voice outside said. "Yuh want all the neighbors t' gather around to enquire about what we're doin' with all their best horses?"

"There's a dog in here, growlin' at me," the man with the light complained.

"Well, shag him out and let's get on about our business. We don't want to be here all night!"

The horse thief swung his rope end timidly and spoke to the dog. "Git outta there, Rover, Ring, Rags, Shep, or whatever yore name is! Beat it! Git!" he said in a quavery voice.

The dog crouched between the pony's legs

12

and snarled back at the man, who hesitated in the doorway, patting his feet this way and that but coming no nearer.

"Aw, Tige — Tippie — Towser — git outta there, PLEASE!" the man said, flapping his hands and the rope end in the general direction of the dog, who was now on his feet.

But the dog just stood between the pony's front legs with his hackles raised and stared back at the horse thief and growled.

"It's that dog that follered us from the last place back there," the man whined. "An' he don't take kindly to bein' shagged out. He's wearin' his hair turned wrongside out, an' his eyes is shinin' red, an' he's showin' his tushes clean back to his throat! Some of you fellers come in here an' shag him out if yuh wantta, but I'm quittin' the job right now. I never did git along with dogs, nohow!"

"Leave him in there, then!" said the weary voice outside. "But whatever you're goin' to do, git busy an' do it, an' don't stand there all night augurin' about it! We got a long way to go before daylight!"

The timid horse thief led the new horse inside and tied him, keeping a wary eye on the dog and complaining constantly in a small, sad voice. As soon as he was finished he hustled down the ramp to the ground, leaving the dog and the pony inside together.

The doors were shut quickly and the ramp put back up. The horses braced themselves against the swaying and rocking of the truck as it started off, grinding and bumping over the rough roads.

The horse thieves traveled all night, stealthily working their way out of the country by the little-used roads that wound across the big fenced pastures. Every mile or so there were stout wire gates barring their way. These they closed carefully after going through, to leave no sign of their passing. Most of the time they drove without lights so as not to attract the attention of the scattered ranches they passed. The wheel tracks showed as dark lines against the pale gleam of the grass in the moonlight.

After the first few miles the horses accustomed

themselves to the swaying of the truck and rode quietly. Now and again the dog got up from where he lay between the pony's feet to sniff at the cracks in the van body, trying to learn something of what was outside. He'd sniff a while, and claw a little to try and widen the crack, then lie down again at the pony's feet.

The roads wound around black buttes and over rolling hills that grew steeper and more broken as the night went on. Daylight found the horse thieves in some very rough country not far from the rim of the badlands. Just after sunup they drove the creaking and protesting van carefully down a deeply rutted and washed-out old road into a hollow which hid some tumbledown corrals and buildings that showed signs of having been long deserted.

They drove into one of the corrals and parked close beside an old shed. After the corral gate was closed they opened the doors and let down the ramp to unload the horses.

It was the thieves' habit, when they were hauling stolen horses, to travel at night and lay up

15

during the day. This place was well hidden, so they had fixed up the well and the corral and used it regularly for a hideout.

One man pumped water into the trough by the fence. The horse thief that didn't like dogs went up the ramp to untie the horses and hand out the lead ropes to the men on the ground. When he came to the spotted pony, the dog growled and the man jumped back like he'd been snakebit.

"I clean forgot about that dog bein' in there!" he called out in some excitement. "Reckon he'll bite me?"

"Naw," the others told him. "Jest don't make any sudden moves whilst yuh lead the horse out and the dog most likely won't bother yuh none. Anyways, a dogbite don't amount to much. I been dogbit plenty of times."

"Well, I never been dogbit, an' I'm not achin' to be, neither, if yuh care to know how I feel about it!" the timid horse thief said. As he backed down the ramp, he held the spotted pony's lead rope by the very end.

The pony tapped and snorted his way care-

16

fully down the ramp with the dog walking stiff-legged beside him, showing his teeth at the men. When the pony's halter was unbuckled he followed the dog away to the far side of the corral and stood sniffing and snorting. The dog made a quick circuit of the corral to see if there was any way out. After he'd satisfied himself that the gates were all closed and the fence solid he came back and lay down by the pony's feet. The other horses were drinking at the trough, where one of the horse thieves was pumping water.

When the others had all finished and were rolling in the deep dust of the old corral, the dog got up, stretched, and after touching noses with the pony led the way to the trough. The pony smelled around the edge suspiciously until he heard the dog's noisy lapping, then he plunged his own muzzle deep into the water and drank thirstily. After he had his fill he followed the dog back to the corner of the corral, well away from the other horses.

The horse thief who had been pumping water watched them a while, then spoke up. "I've

17

seen dogs foller horses now and again," he said. "But I don't ever remember seein' a horse foller a dog before. Notice how that spotted pony don't move nowhere unless the dog is with him?"

"Reckon there's right smart you've never seen, when it comes to that," another one told him. "Let's go git some coffee."

Over by the truck the thieves had made a cookfire by pouring gasoline on a pile of dry sand, and had gotten out a grub box and a skillet and coffee pot. With bacon, eggs, and store bread they were making breakfast. When all had eaten, one of them went up to the top of a nearby hill to keep watch, and the rest got out pieces of canvas and blankets and hunted places under the truck or inside the shed to sleep.

Hideout

All day the place was quiet except for the stamping of the horses or the snoring of the horse thieves. Flies buzzed, and magpies squalled and quarreled in nearby plum thickets. At intervals whoever was on lookout would come down and wake a man to take his place, but that was the only movement to be seen. The spotted pony stood on three legs and dozed. The dog stretched out in his shadow and napped lightly, waking every time a horse thief stirred.

Late in the afternoon one of the men crawled out from under the truck and went to the trough and splashed water on his face. He stood around a while looking at the horses and scratching himself, then got the coffee pot and filled it with fresh water and relit the fire. Before long the others came out and started digging cans of tomatoes and sardines and cheese and crackers out of the grub box while they waited for the coffee to boil. They sat around and ate and talked sleepily, for there was no hurry, darkness being some hours away yet.

The boss horse thief had been sitting a little way off from the rest, watching the horses and spearing peaches out of a can with his knife as he figured his possible profits. He watched closely while the pony followed the dog to the water trough for another drink.

"Yuh know, boys," he said after a little, "it strikes me there's somethin' queer about that spotted pony. I don't know what it is, but somehow he don't act jest right."

"That's jest what I said this mornin'!" one of the men said.

"Aw, he's jest feelin' snorty because he's in a strange place, that's all that's the matter with him!" another horse thief allowed.

"It's somethin' more than that," the boss insisted, spearing another peach. "One of yuh fellers catch him up an' let me look him over close."

While one of the horse thieves was putting a

20

halter on the pony the dog stiffened out his tail and growled. The man paid no attention and led the pony over to the boss while the dog stood a little way off, watching suspiciously.

The boss walked all round the pony, picking up his feet and feeling his legs, whistling a small sad tune the while.

"He looks good, all right," he admitted as he stepped back and scratched himself thoughtfully. "I can't find anythin' wrong with him an' he looks like as fancy a hoss as we've stole yet. But I still can't git it out of my head that somethin' about him isn't jest right. Lead him around some so I can see how he moves."

The pony stepped out free and dainty, his head up and his ears pointed.

"Yessir, by doggies he does look good!" the boss said after he'd watched the pony circle the corral a couple of times. "Mebbe I'll keep him myself. Bring him on back."

As the pony was led toward the boss horse thief he stepped on the coffee pot and smashed it flat, and when he jumped back, snorting and rearing, he stumbled into the cookfire. As the

rope was jerked out of the horse thief's hands, the dog darted past him to where the pony stood, braced and trembling.

"Now what in the world made him do a thing like that?" the boss wanted to know. "That thing was out in plain sight. I wonder . . ." And he walked carefully up talking quietly to both the pony and the growling dog between his front legs. He looked closely at the pony's eyes, turning the lids back and flicking his hands over his face. Then he stepped back and pushed his hat onto the back of his head.

"Joe!" he bellowed. "Come here, yuh chuckleheaded scissorbill! An' come a-runnin'!"

"What's the fuss about, Boss?" Joe asked as he sidled up.

"What's the fuss about?" the boss hollered, turning red and swelling up like a turkey gobbler. "There's plenty of fuss! Yuh picked a blind hoss for us to steal, that's what's the fuss! Ain't it enough?"

"Aw, Boss, that hoss ain't blind," Joe whined. "I seen the kid that owns him ridin' him lots

of times. Yuh know I wouldn't pick no blind hoss to steal."

"Don't tell me he ain't blind!" the boss told him. "Watch this." He flicked his hand in front of the pony's eyes. "Notice he don't bat an eyelash!"

"Well, I'll be dogged!" said Joe, sidling off a little. "It's like I told yuh, Boss; I seen the kid ridin' him, an' he shore didn't act blind."

"That must be why the dog sticks so clost to him," another horse thief said. "Yuh remember this mornin' I told yuh I'd never seen a hoss foller a dog like that pony was doin'."

"Yuh mean the dog leads the horse around like a blind man?" another man asked.

"Looks like it," the boss said. "Yuh noticed he didn't have no trouble until yuh led him around without the dog."

"I never did hear of such a thing," Joe said.

"I never hear of a case jest like this, myself," another thief said. "But yuh can never tell jest what a horse will take up with. Feller I know one time has him a race horse that won't eat or do

23

anythin' without a pet goat is with him in the stall. Another feller has a horse that takes up with a Banty rooster. The chicken lives in his stall an' rides with him in the truck whenever they move. Otherwise they can't do nothin' with the horse."

"This is all very well," the boss put in, "but what we goin' to do with this blind crittur Joe got us stuck with? If we was runnin' a dog an' pony show we might be able to use him, but in the horse-stealin' business I don't rightly see what we can do with him."

The horse thieves stood around thinking that over, and their comments about what they thought of a man that would pick out a blind horse to steal didn't make Joe feel any better.

"Boss," he said, "with the dog helpin' him that hoss fooled us. Don't yuh reckon he'd fool a buyer? At least long enough fer us to be gone somewheres else?"

"He might," the boss agreed, "but we can't afford to do business that way. If we was honest hoss traders, now, we could afford to cheat folks dealin' with us. We'd be almost expected to, for that matter. But bein' as we're hoss thieves we have to be honest in our dealin's, so folks won't git to enquirin' too close into our affairs."

"Yeah, the Boss is right!" one man said.

"We'll have to turn him loose," the boss decided. "I been studyin' about it whilst you fellers been chawin' the rag, and I've elected Joe t' lead him up to the rimrock an' turn him loose — other side of the drift fence, where he can get down into the badlands."

"Aw Boss — " Joe started to say.

"Git goin', Joe," the boss told him. "It was you got us into this jackpot, so you can see to gettin' rid of him."

"But why can't we jest turn him loose here, or shoot him?" Joe wanted to know. "It's a long walk up there to the rimrock!"

"If we turn him out here," the boss explained, "somebody will sooner or later find him an' begin to wonder how he got here. We can't afford to have folks nosin' round this hideout of ours, as you know right well. It's all open country over the rimrock, an' he'll either go back to the wild bunch or break his neck in a washout. In either

case it'll be a long time before anyone finds him, an' that'll save us considerable embarrassment."

"Yessir!" Joe said. He picked up the pony's lead rope, keeping one eye on the dog, who was growling at him.

"An' another thing, Joe," the boss added. "Reckon it's only fair you work for nothin' this trip. This deal has cost us money, an' it don't seem fair that the other boys should suffer by it. An' maybe gettin' no share of the money will make yuh more careful about the kind of hosses yuh pick fer us to steal from now on!"

Joe didn't say anything more out loud, but he muttered hair-raising things as he led the pony away, kicking at every rock and bush that came in his reach. By the time he'd found the gate in the drift fence, which was more than a mile from the truck, he was hot and tired and his feet were hurting him something dreadful. High-heeled boots are not made for walking.

He took the halter off the pony, then aimed a mighty kick at the dog to relieve his feelings. That was a big mistake, for the dog was in no good humor himself, and had taken a great dis-

like to the horse thief from the very beginning. He dodged the kick and grabbed the man by the seat of his pants. Joe yelled and tried to get away, but the dog hung on, growling and snarling until he'd torn a big piece out of the horse thief's pants.

As soon as he got loose Joe grabbed his hat and hurried away as fast as he could hobble on his sore feet. The last the dog saw of him he had thrown his hat on the ground and was stomping it and kicking it along ahead of him, swearing horribly the while.

Drift Fence

The dog stood growling until the horse thief was out of sight, then he trotted over to where the blind pony had circled a little way off and was waiting for him. After he'd sniffed the pony's nose and around his feet, he lay down in the grass and panted. The pony stood close to him, stamping uneasily and waiting for the dog to decide what to do next.

Ordinarily a horse that is turned loose in strange territory will drift back home as soon as possible, but the horse thieves had come a roundabout way and there were many wire fences with tight gates between this place and the ranch. Of course, the dog could have taken off straight across country and been home in a day or two, for the fences were no trouble to him. But he had been leading the blind pony around for a long time, and had no idea of leaving him now.

It had all started the year before when the boy had noticed the pony with the fancy spots, and the strange hoodlike marking on his face, among some horses that had drifted into the ranch. He had persuaded the old cowboy to keep him when the other horses were turned back on the range. After they'd roped him they'd found he was stone blind, but by then the boy was so pleased with the odd looking colt that he wanted to keep him anyway. They turned him into the pasture with the other saddle horses.

At first the pony had been frightened and lonely in his new surroundings. On the range where he'd been born he'd had his mother and the other horses and colts in the band to keep him company. By listening closely as he followed them, he could pretty well know what was ahead of him, and so avoid accidents. But in the pasture where all the horses were strange and unfriendly, it had seemed that every time he turned around or took a step he bumped into a post or fence or some such unfamiliar thing. The windmill had frightened him with its creaking and clanking, and for a while he was afraid to go up to the tank

for water. And when he tried to make up with the other horses they lashed out with heels or teeth and drove him off.

Much of the time the boy and the old cowpuncher were riding about the ranch affairs and the dog was left alone, for no cowboy lets a dog follow when he rides. For some reason the dog began to spend more and more time down in the pasture near the blind pony. At first the furry smell and panting sounds of the dog, and even the padding of his paws as he trotted around, reminded the pony of the wolves he'd feared so much on the range. But after a time he noticed that neither the boy nor the other horses paid the strange creature any notice, so he lost his fear.

The dog seemed somehow to know the pony was blind, and before long he had set himself up as his guide, trotting along a little to one side or just under the pony's nose as they went from place to place. The pony soon learned to depend on the dog, and followed him by listening to the sound of his paws, the swishing of his bushy tail, and the other small sounds he made.

The dog had come to take great pride in this job of his, and would trot along with his ears cocked up at an alert angle and his tail curled rakishly over his back as he led the pony from the pasture to the windmill and back, or went on small trips, searching out the best grazing for the pony.

And later, when the boy had started breaking and training the pony, the dog had stayed close by, watching everything that was done. If the pony balked or snorted at a new piece of equipment, the dog would sniff loudly and busily around it until he'd made sure it was harmless. Then he'd touch noses with the pony and the lesson would go on. If for some reason the dog happened to be gone for a little time, the pony would become restless and fretful, whinnying and stamping until he came back.

So now he stood and sniffed the strange smells in the little wind blowing along the rimrock, and waited for the dog to lead him home.

Soon the dog got up and stretched and yawned and looked around him. A little way off was the drift fence they had just been brought through, barring the way home. It wound along, more or less at right angles to the way they wanted to go, following the rim of the badlands. Although the dog didn't know it, the fence ran for miles in either direction, having been built to keep stock in the badlands from drifting out onto the grasslands around the ranches in the open country. There was a space of thirty to a hundred yards between the fence and the rimrock, and drifting horses and cattle had worn deep paths in this open space as they followed the windings of the fence.

Every now and again a trail branched off, leading down into the unfenced, broken country below. From where the dog stood he could see, far below him, the white alkali flats crisscrossed with cattle trails leading to waterholes around the springs and sinks in the side canyons. Wind and rain-worn buttes and pinnacles, in odd castle shapes, stood from the bare flats, or ran out like rows of enormous teeth from canyon walls that were gray and pink and black and yellow in color.

After he'd looked and sniffed all round the dog led the way back to the fence. While the pony leaned against the wire and pointed his ears toward home, the dog prowled along the fence, carefully sniffing the fence posts to read the sign of any dogs or coyotes that might have passed, and looking for a gate they could get through, or a corner they could go around. When he found nothing, he went back to the colt and worked along the fence in the other direction. But he had no better luck that way, so he trotted out to the edge of the hill.

He sat for some time looking back in the direction of the horse thieves' hideout, but saw nothing moving. The pony whinnied nervously, so he trotted back to where he still leaned against the gate.

The dog sat near the pony and listened to the sad and fretful sound of the long-billed brown curlews and the quarreling of the magpies down below the rimrock. Now and again he touched noses with the pony, or whined to himself, for he was hungry and thirsty as well as lonely.

The pony leaned against the wire gate or shuffled a few steps along the fence in either direction. Sometimes he'd graze a little way off, but soon he'd come back to the fence again. Occasionally he'd throw up his head and whinny shrilly, then hold his breath as he listened for some answer.

It began to get dark. A meadow lark perched on a nearby fence post to sing a little before bedding down in the grass for the night. The jack rabbits and bull bats came out. Down below, the badlands were dark except where a pinnacle stuck up high enough to catch the last light. But the dog and the blind pony still paced the fence. They'd travel a little way, then come back to the gate, hoping that somehow they'd find it open at last so they could go through.

During the night neither one slept much. The dog was used to the familiar sights and sounds of the ranch, and here the wind made strange and lonely noises as it blew into the gulleys and canyons below. He heard coyotes yapping far off, and small animals of one kind and another making small rustling noises out in the dark. The pony had known these noises when he was a colt on the range, but then he'd always had other horses near him for comfort and company, so now he too was restless and spooky. Whenever he moved the dog got up from the grass and followed him, or took a quick circle around to see what was near.

All the next morning they stayed in sight of the fence, but along toward the middle of the day the dog, who had been watching strings of cattle crossing the flats below on the way to water, would trot off a way toward a trail that led down off the rimrock, then stop and whine for the pony to follow. After several false starts, he got the pony to start drifting toward water. And, finally, the dog led the way carefully along one of the well-worn trails to the flats below.

The trail had been worn deep from years of use by cattle and horses, and probably buffalo in the old days, on the way down to water. It wound past deep washouts and cut-banks, across gulleys and around strangely shaped walls and buttes for a mile or more before it came out on the flat floor of a dry canyon. Smaller washes and gulches opened into the bigger canyon, and before long they came to water, where a chain of little seeps from a spring in a nearby box canyon crossed the trail.

The pony listened to the dog sniffing around the edge of a little pool, and heard him wade into it and start lapping greedily. He stamped and snorted, testing the footing carefully before he ventured up to drink beside the dog.

Then the pony grazed on the level canyon floor, and the dog prowled around the choke-cherry and the buffalo-berry thickets along the cut-banks, in the hope of stirring out a rabbit or something else to eat. He found a number of fresh holes where skunks had dug up mice or ground squirrels, and, scattered around another place, a few small tufts of fur where a coyote had eaten a rabbit, but there wasn't a taste left for him. Sniffing farther on, he saw where a shrike had pinned a small bird to a thorn on a buffalo-berry bush and gone away and left it. The dog walked around under the bush, eyeing the dead bird, but though he stood on his hind legs, and even tried jumping for it, the branch was too high. He went on, disappointed.

Around a shoulder of the canyon wall, under an overhanging bank, he discovered an old coyote den. The place smelled musty and deserted,

but nonetheless he worked his way cautiously through the bushes until he had examined the entrance from all sides, growling a little, and making sure no badger or skunk had moved in. He looked over the bones of rabbits and other small animals that lay around the den mouth. But they had been there so long they were polished white by the weather and the ants, so were no use to him at all.

He smelled around the den and finally crawled into it and scratched round in the litter on the floor. A long-tailed deer mouse jumped out from under his paw when he turned over its nest. The dog made a frantic snap at the mouse, but he'd been taken by surprise and the mouse disappeared safely into a crevice at the back of the den. The dog tried to dig it out, snuffling and whining hungrily at the hole, but soon gave it up as hopeless. He went back and tore the abandoned nest apart, scattering the store of grass seeds it contained and sniffing loudly at the warm mouse smell. But the seeds were no good to him, and as he was unable to find any more mice, he crawled back out.

By one of the pools a garter snake, hunting frogs, slithered ahead of him, but he didn't care for snakes or frogs. After he'd made sure there was nothing for him to eat in the canyon he drank again and lay down near the pony, who was now resting in the shade.

Later, when the heat of the day was past and the shadows had begun to lengthen out in long black strips from the buttes, they went back up the trail to the rimrock and idled along the fence near the gate. The pony spent much of his time there, leaning over the wire, pointing his head and ears toward the ranch, and whinnying often.

They stayed in the neighborhood for several days, going down to the seeps for water once a day, but always coming back to the fence in the hope the gate might be open. Sometimes they drifted one direction or the other along the fence, but never went very far.

There was good grass there so the pony did all right, but the dog got hungrier and hungrier, for he'd never learned to hunt as the coyotes do. He was beginning to look very gaunt and ragged when the pony happened to step on a meadow lark's nest one day, breaking some of the eggs. The dog lost no time licking up the broken eggs, and polishing out the shells. He wasn't, normally, an egg-sucking dog, but he started worrying the unbroken eggs and soon learned he could open them and eat out the inside.

From then on he learned fast, and searched the grass and bushes most of his spare time. He learned that when a bird fluttered along the ground ahead of him, acting crippled, there was a nest nearby and that the bird was just tolling him away, and would fly off as soon as he'd followed it a safe distance. So he soon ignored the fluttering birds and searched back for the nest, finding a good many that way.

Another day, seeing something moving the thick grass in a little draw, he pounced and caught a field mouse. From then on he would sit quiet in places he learned might have mice, waiting for the grass to move, and soon became almost as good as a coyote at mouse hunting. He also learned, when he'd chased a ground squirrel into a hole, to lie quietly, hidden by a tuft of grass or sage brush, until the squirrel popped his head back out to look around.

The moon was coming up earlier each night, and the bright moonlight made both the dog and the pony restless. They began to wander farther and farther from the gate, along the drift fence. One day, going down off the rimrock for water, they came to a trail that led them to water some miles from the seeps where they had been watering. Cattle trails are like old buffalo trails, winding in roundabout ways to find the easiest grade, so when they came back on top of the rimrock they were in a part of the country they'd never seen before. The drift fence was there, still barring their way, but the gate was miles away and they never went back to it.

They didn't travel steadily or with any plan. Sometimes they'd stay several days near a fence corner where the fence changed direction, going down to water and coming back up the same trail. Again they'd stay down on the flats for several days, if the grazing was good and there were plenty of mice and birds' nests to keep the dog

fed and busy. Then something would disturb
them or the pony would become restless, and
the dog would guide him back to a trail leading
in the general direction of the rimrock and the
fence.

Washout

Whenever they traveled the dog kept a close watch on the blind pony, to see that nothing happened to him. On the trails from the rimrock to the canyons below he was especially careful, for there were washouts and cut-banks on all sides that a horse could fall into or over. The pony seemed to realize this, for around the sharp twists and turns he kept his muzzle down almost touching the dog's bushy tail.

Also, the pony was remembering the things he'd learned on the range as a colt, depending on his nose to tell him much about what was near. When he smelled chokecherry and buffalo-berry bushes he knew there were probably gulleys and cut-banks, for those things seldom grew on the flat. The sharp clean smell of ground juniper, or creeping cedar, warned him of the outcroppings of rocks it grew on. The boggy ground that could suck down a horse's hoofs and trap him had a sharp alkali smell that warned the pony away while the ground under his feet was still firm. When he smelled sage the ground was usually flat with only the tough, twisted bushes themselves to watch out for.

Even the prairie-dog towns, with their hundreds of burrows that a horse could break a leg in, had a faint but distinctive smell, a mixture of dust and the oily smell of the prairie dogs themselves, to warn him even if their barking didn't. The bigger badger holes smelled musty and rank. The smell of overripe cucumber told him of rattlesnakes curled up under shade during the day or traveling about during the night hunting. These things and a hundred others that the ordinary horse never noticed, the blind pony paid close attention to. Still, it was mainly the dog he depended on.

Days when they were not searching the fence for a way home the dog would lead the pony out on the flats in the morning until they found a place where the grass was good. If he seemed satisfied to graze quietly and there was nothing dangerous nearby, the dog would prowl around on little excursions of his own. He'd search the buck-brush thickets for birds' eggs and small rabbits. Once in a while he'd find an old sun-dried carcass that he could gnaw on for a while, although they were usually so iron hard the time was wasted. He soon learned to look under any cottonwood or box elder tree that seemed to have a hawk or an owl's nest in it, for sometimes parts of small carcasses fell on the ground.

And there were the tracks of passing coyotes and other animals to be investigated. He got the surprise of his life one day when he went up to what appeared to be a regular sniffing place for coyotes and found that a gray wolf had been there only a few hours before. He stood on the tips of his toes and looked all around, growling, with his hair bristled out and his teeth showing clear back to the hinge of his jaw. But he didn't neglect to leave word of his own visit before he hurried back to the blind pony to make sure he was all right.

When the pony tired of a place and started acting restless the dog would lead him off. Some-

times as they were moving from one place to another the dog would see something he had to at-
tend to right away, such as digging a while at a
gopher hole or some such thing. If they were on
level ground the pony would graze until the dog
was ready to go on, but if there were washouts or
cut-banks around he'd stand quietly and wait
on the trail.

On hot days they'd climb up on top of a nearby
hill toward the middle of the day, where they
could get what breeze there might be to blow the
flies away. Through the hot afternoon the pony
would stand and doze, drowsily switching flies,
while the dog stretched out in his shadow and
slept or gnawed at the thorns in his paws. Toward
evening, when the shadows began to stretch out
long and black across the flats, they'd shake
themselves awake, and go down to the flats
again.

One night a heavy rainstorm caught them going down off the rimrock looking for shelter
from the cold wind that had come up about sundown. In a few minutes the trail was slippery as
grease, and streams of water ran down the gulleys

45

of the eroded canyon walls, washing rocks and lumps of clay underfoot. The rain beat down on the dog and pony in sheets, and in places the water in the path was fetlock deep. The pony inched along behind the dog, feeling out the ground carefully ahead of each hoof before he set it down in the swirling water. Often, when he set a foot down he could feel the clay washing out from under it as the running water cut new gulleys down the path.

As they worked their way along an especially narrow shelf against a steep wall a part of the bank above caved off, sending a heavy mass of dirt sliding and tumbling down against the pony's feet. He snorted and plunged ahead to try to regain his footing, but slipped over the edge of the trail instead.

He fell only a few feet, rolled over in deep mud, and managed to get up unharmed. He was shaken and badly frightened as he stamped and whinnied for the dog. The dog whined in answer, and scrambled down from the trail into the washout beside him. The pony soon quieted and stood where he was while the dog investigated

the place they were in. The sides were higher than the pony's head. There was no way out except for a small tunnel about the size of a badger hole at the bottom of the bank on the side away from the trail. It was like being in a tub some twenty feet across and six or eight feet deep. Water was pouring in off the trail, but it ran out again through the tunnel on the other side.

The dog found that one of the banks wasn't as steep as the others. He ran up without much difficulty, and turned and whined for the pony to follow. But the pony's greater weight and sharp hoofs caved the muddy bank every time he tried to scramble up, throwing him back to the bottom. The dog ran back and forth on the trail above, whining and worrying as the pony tried time after time to climb the bank. Finally the pony gave up and stood with his feet braced in the mud, shivering and snorting.

The dog slid back down the bank and stayed with him for a while, but the water and mud were inches deep so after a time he climbed back to the trail and lay there shivering and whimpering. It was a cold and miserable night for both of

47

them. The rain finally stopped, but the wind blew down from the rimrock sharp and chilly against their wet hides.

In the morning when the sun came up and warmed them a little the pony tramped round and round in the drying mud at the bottom of the washout, or tried now and again to scramble out.

After watching him a while the dog started searching the nearby gulleys for something to eat, as he did in all his spare time. He heard some magpies quarreling and raising a great fuss over a part of a rabbit carcass they'd found, so he went over and drove them off. He carried the prize back to the edge of the washout where he lay and ate it while he kept an eye on the pony below. After he'd finished it he lay on the trail and gnawed at burrs in his coat, and cleaned his paws of the lumps of mud that had collected between the pads.

Every now and again he got up and trotted around the washout, whining for the pony, who would try to climb the muddy bank to him.

As the sun came out warmer and warmer the ground began to dry out, and by noon the banks of the washout were firm enough for the pony to scramble up the caved side and join the dog. He stood snorting and blowing while the dog fussed happily around him. After a while he got his wind back, and the dog led the way carefully and slowly on down the trail. For some days after that they stayed on the flats below, and avoided all the trails to the higher ground.

Wild Horses

One afternoon as the blind pony and the dog made their way along a deep-worn trail leading to some seeps where they had watered several times before, the dog noticed a horse on the skyline not far off. It was a mustang stallion standing watch while the mares and colts in his band drank.

This was the first time since the dog and the pony had been turned through the drift fence that they'd seen other horses close by. Several times when they were on the rimrock the dog had seen a band or two moving across the flats below. And now and again in the heat of the day he had noticed others standing on some ridge far off. But they'd been too far away for the pony to hear or smell them, and the dog wasn't particu-

larly interested, as he was lonely for the ranch and not for other horses.

The pony could not see the stallion on the hogback, but when he winded the mares and colts watering at the seeps he stopped and threw up his head, listening and sniffing. He could hear the horses stamping, along with the noisy sound of their drinking, and the occasional squeal or thud of hoofs on ribs as they settled small differences among themselves.

The pony whinnied and started crowding the dog's heels in his hurry to get ahead. Around a turn in the trail they came in sight of the water. The dog saw there were ten or twelve mares and colts drinking there, and stopped to look the situation over. But the pony whinnied again and hurried on ahead without waiting for the dog.

He came up to the drinking range horses, whickering softly, and tried to crowd up close to one of the old mares, sniffing her and nuzzling her side. She squealed and let fly with her heels, jarring his ribs. While he stood back trying to make up his mind what to do next the stallion came lop-

51

ing up to chase him off, slashing him on shoulder and hip with his strong yellow teeth.

As soon as the stallion turned back the dog went to the pony and led him off a little distance, where they stood and waited for the horses to finish drinking.

When they had all finished the stallion rounded them up and started them away up the trail. The pony heard them moving out and threw up his head and whinnied to them. When they didn't answer he started to follow, but the stallion whirled and trumpeted warningly, so he turned back to where the dog stood waiting.

The pony listened, whinnying occasionally, until he could no longer hear the horses on the trail, then went with the dog to drink. For a while he grazed around, finding a tuft of grass here and another there that the others had missed, while the dog tried to dig out a picket-pin gopher. The dog would dig frantically, whining and grunting to himself, then he'd stick his head as far into the hole as he could and snuffle and slobber while he assured himself the gopher was still home. He worked until he had a hole he could get his whole head and shoulders into, but the gopher dug faster than he could, in the other direction, so he gave up.

By that time the pony had stopped trying to graze and had sniffed out the trail of the mustangs, and followed it a little way. As soon as he heard the dog shake the dirt out of his fur and come trotting up he started away up the trail, his nose down, searching for tracks of the range horses. There was nothing for the dog to do but lead the way, even though it was not the direction he wanted to go. They traveled steadily for a couple of hours with the pony smelling out the trail at every fork and turn, following the wild horses on their way to the better grass on the high flats. Every so often the pony would stop and whinny, then hold his breath while he listened for an answer. While he did that the dog would sit panting, looking back the way they'd come and whining when he thought of the ranch, which was in that direction.

After a time they came out on a ridge and the

dog saw the horses scattered out on the flat below, grazing and resting. An old mare standing lookout on a little knoll threw up her head and whinnied warningly when she saw the dog and the strange pony on the skyline. The stallion answered her, bowing his neck and trotting up from where he'd been grazing on the other side of the band. Coming between his mares and colts and the strangers, he stopped and whistled a warning.

The pony stopped, listening, and whickered softly to himself while the dog whined and tried to lead him back the way they'd come. But the pony started forward again. The stallion laid back his ears and thundered up to chase him off, squealing and biting and lashing out with forefeet and heels.

The pony was slashed and bruised in a dozen places when the stallion finally trotted back to join the other horses. The dog padded up to the trembling pony and touched noses with him and sniffed around a trickle of blood that ran down one front leg from a gash the stallion's teeth had made in his shoulder. He whined softly and tried to lead him away, but without success.

54

The rest of the afternoon the pony grazed as close to the range horses as he dared, stopping now and again to listen and whinny to them. Several times he even tried to edge closer, but the stallion grazed watchfully between him and the other horses, and warned him off whenever he came close.

All the next morning the pony stayed within hearing of the wild horse band. After chasing him away several times when he had hopefully tried to join them, the stallion suddenly bunched the mares and colts and drove them off straight across the broken country. He brought up the rear himself, nipping and crowding the stragglers until the whole band broke into a rapid trot. The pony could hear them leaving and tried to follow, but there was no trail across the many gulleys and ditches in that direction. He had to travel so slowly, even with the dog leading him, that he was soon left far behind.

After he'd given up following the wild bunch the pony grazed, stopping at times to listen and to whinny in the direction the horses had gone. The dog tried to lead him back, but it was almost

evening before the pony was willing to follow him. The dog turned onto the first trail he came to that seemed to lead back in the general direction of the ranch, and they traveled steadily until after dark, when they came to a water hole in a little cedar canyon.

They spent the night there. The next morning the colt was stiff and sore from the punishment he'd taken the day before, and was unwilling to leave. Instead, he grazed around on the close-cropped slopes and ridges nearby, keeping always in hearing distance of the water hole.

Whenever one of the mustang bands came to water he tried to join them. But always the result was the same. If a stallion didn't run him off, the mares bit and kicked him until he was driven away. And when the strange horses had watered they moved back up the trails they'd come down without a backward look at the lonesome pony, no matter how loudly he whinnied after them.

Meanwhile the dog discovered that there were young jack rabbits in the sagebrush nearby, and stalked them, creeping slowly across the open places with his belly dragging the ground like a hunting coyote's, until he was close enough to make his rush. He missed more often than not, but now and then he did make a meal, so while he looked very ragged and gaunt he was managing to keep from starving.

His feet had begun to bother him. Cactus thorns stuck in his pads, broke off and festered, and small burrs and cactus lodged in the hair between his toes. Much of the country was bare of grass and baked hard by the sun, holding heat like a stove lid, so his paws dried and cracked and the pads wore down until they were sore and raw. Much of his time was spent licking and gnawing at the sore places.

Early mornings and late evenings small birds came in flocks to the water hole under the little scrubby cedars. And the big sage chickens walked down from the flats in long, dignified-looking files, making quiet talking sounds among themselves. They drank in formation, then walked away to their dusting places, or to where they'd bed down for the night under the sagebrush.

Around the edges of the water hole where the mud had dried hard, salt-hungry animals came to lick and gnaw at the white alkali coating. One morning the dog saw a band of antelope there. As soon as he came close they bounced away, flashing their white rump patches and circling single file to the top of a small hill nearby, where they stood for a while, watching the dog curiously.

Later, while the dog was poking through some buckbrush patches looking for birds' nests or mice, he came upon an antelope fawn lying where the mother had hidden it. He bumped into the fawn only by accident, for its scent was so faint and it lay so still, with its head and neck stretched out on the ground and its ears plastered flat against its neck, that it was almost invisible. The big dog was puzzled by its stillness. He felt sure this must be an animal of some kind, but when he nosed round it and smelled it all over the fawn never flinched. He tried licking its face in an experimental sort of way, and still the fawn didn't even blink an eye. He sat down with his tongue hanging out and watched it. After a while, he whined, and then growled a little, but still the creature didn't move.

Once a fawn is hidden, he almost never stirs until the old one comes, depending upon his spots and his stillness to make him invisible. After sniffing the strange animal all over again the dog went away, but looked over his shoulder at intervals to see if it moved.

At the top of the nearby ridge the dog met the old antelope coming back to her fawn. She lowered her head and stamped and snorted threateningly, and sidled toward him. The dog growled and started to trot away, but as soon as he turned his back she made a run for him. When he stopped and turned on her, bristling and growling, she slowed down, but kept on crowding him and crowding him until he moved slowly on. They traveled for some distance in this fashion, with the dog edging slowly away but not daring to turn his back. An antelope's hoofs are razor sharp and can cut a dog or coyote to ribbons. When they were well out of sight of the place where the fawn was hidden the antelope turned back and the dog, much relieved, hurried to where he'd left the blind pony.

Later in the day the pony gave up trying to join the unfriendly bands of range horses, and let the dog lead him toward the rimrock again.

Range Cattle

Sometimes during the days the dog and the blind pony had been in and out of the badlands, the dog had seen bunches of range cattle grazing, or strung out on the way to water, and had made it a point to avoid them.

But one hot afternoon he was lying in the pony's shadow, gnawing a thorn in his foot and resting, when a long line of range cattle came drifting down the trail. They passed close by, walking steadily along in single file. The leaders paid no attention to the colt, for cattle are used to seeing horses, and they didn't at first notice the dog.

He'd been sleepily listening to a magpie scolding from a nearby bush when he heard the rattling of the cattle's feet. He had flattened his ears back against his head and crouched close to the ground, watching, hoping they'd not notice him.

But an old cow in the middle of the string happened to catch his scent and stopped, throwing up her head and spreading her big ears wide as she tried to locate him.

As soon as the line of cattle stopped, alarmed by the old cow's actions, the dog got up and nervously moved around to the other side of the colt. When he moved, the cattle saw him and began bawling and surging around, for a dog is a strange and fearsome thing to them. They gathered in a wide circle around the colt and the dog, bawling, pawing up dust and rattling their horns. Slowly the steers and the old cows without calves crowded in closer and closer. The cows outside the circle took up the bawling, and added to the uproar. The pony was frightened by this confusion he couldn't see and snorted and stamped, turning this way and that. But whichever way he turned he could hear the heavy breathing of the angry cattle facing him. The dog skulked beside the pony and bristled and growled.

Every now and again some warlike old cow, after bellowing and pawing up dirt, would wring

her tail up over her back and make a rush for the dog. But the pony, hearing her come, would whirl and lash out with his front feet or his heels, and the cow would swagger back to her place in the circle.

The ring of heads and horns got smaller and smaller as the cattle grew bolder and crowded closer in upon the dog and the blind pony. The dog backed farther and farther under the pony, only darting out now and then to snap at a cow's nose, for he realized that without the pony's protection the cattle would trample him down in short order.

The cattle milled around all afternoon, bawling and raising a dust that could be seen for miles. At times they'd lose interest and the circle would open out as some went off to drink and others began to graze. But as soon as the dog moved to lead the pony away, some red-eyed old cow would bawl and make a rush for him, bringing the whole herd round again.

Toward sundown, however, the cows with calves started drifting away and others followed until there was only one especially belligerent old bobtailed cow left. She stayed close, fussing and worrying and making little rushes at the dog whenever he stirred. His temper hadn't been improved by the afternoon's experience, and he watched her from where he lay between the pony's forefeet, growling a little and his eyes showing red. Sometime after the last steer had disappeared over the ridge the cow made another rush at the dog and got the surprise of a lifetime.

One cow alone the dog wasn't afraid of, so he came snarling and roaring out to meet her, and before she recovered from her astonishment he was snapping and slashing at her tender nose. She whipped her tail straight out behind her, bellowed and whirled away, frantically trying to avoid the maddened dog. When she turned he transferred his attention from her nose to her heels, also very tender. The old cow bawled and bucked and twisted, trying to use her horns on him. But as soon as she faced him, he was back at her nose. She soon gave it up and broke away at a lumbering run. The dog snapped at her heels and flanks until he'd chased her to the top of the ridge.

There he stood watching while the disgusted cow slowed to a flopping trot and went on across the flat, bawling for the rest of the herd. Then the dog sniffed around and kicked the bushes a little before he trotted back to the pony, carrying his tail at a rakish slant and feeling well pleased with himself.

As the moon came up, the dog led the pony away and they traveled a good part of the night.

After that they moved by fits and starts, for both were tired. The pony grazed slowly along, or stood sleeping while the dog prowled nearby. On a little flat he came upon a badger and started to chase him. The badger, in spite of his clumsy look, was fast on his feet and so beat the dog to the den. Once inside he stuck his sharp nose out and growled and snarled, daring the dog to come after him. The dog growled and walked around stiff-legged at a respectful distance for a little, then left. He had learned about badgers the hard way when he was a young and reckless pup, and he had no intention of stirring this grizzled old fellow up.

Early one evening they came to the top of the

rimrock and the fence. During the night a cold drizzly rain came up, and as they were moving along the wire trying to find shelter they came to a gate that was open. The dog led the pony through and they soon came to a brushy draw where there was shelter from the wind for the pony, and where the dog was able to scratch out a dry place under a little overhanging bank.

By morning the rain had stopped. It was just gray light when they stirred out of the draw and started moving again, heading directly toward the home ranch. But before they'd gone a mile they found another fence blocking their way. It was just a big pasture they'd drifted into.

As the pony stood in the fence corner, his head hung over the wire, the dog noticed a ranch house in a draw half a mile away. The dooryard looked deserted, but there was a thin thread of light-colored smoke curling up from the stovepipe where someone had started a breakfast fire.

The dog watched the house, and licked his chops and whined. He looked at the pony, then trotted under the fence and down the hill a way, to sit down and look at the smoke and the ranch

buildings again. When the pony whinnied softly he trotted back and touched noses with him, then started cautiously down the hill toward the house, looking back at the pony now and again to make sure he was all right.

He worked his way to a little knoll behind the corrals, where he sat and looked the place over carefully. While he watched, the kitchen door opened and two ranch dogs were let out. Hunched down on his belly to be less easily seen, the ragged-looking dog watched them start their morning rounds of the place, sniffing fence posts and kicking the sagebrush industriously. He watched as they flushed a big jack rabbit and chased him across the flat, yelping delightedly.

About that time a man came out and set a couple of plates in the yard, then whistled a time or two before he went back inside and closed the door. The stray dog looked at the ranch dogs chasing the rabbit, then slipped around the corral and up to the dooryard, running close to the ground like a hunting coyote. There were flapjacks on the plates and he started gulping them. He'd finished one plate and stepped to the other when the two sleek dogs trotted round the corner of the house, their tails waving and their tongues hanging out. When they saw a strange dog at their breakfast they hauled up short and set up a terrific squalling.

The ragged dog grabbed a last mouthful of flapjacks and streaked across the yard and into the sagebrush without stopping to argue the matter. The ranch dogs were right after him, hollering and blabbering excitedly. But the stray dog saved his breath for running and left them behind. Soon the others turned back to see what was left in their plates.

At a safe distance the dog stopped and finished his breakfast, paying no attention to the big-mouthed ranch dogs barking and bellowing from the dooryard. Then he licked his chops, walked over and kicked the bushes a little, and trotted away with his tail in the air, feeling right satisfied with himself.

He found the blind pony safe where he'd left him, and after he'd touched noses and sniffed round his feet he lay down under the pony's head and worked on the burrs matting his coat while he digested his breakfast. It was the first good meal he'd had in a long time and things looked somewhat brighter than usual.

The pony walked the fence or grazed nearby until late afternoon, when the dog led him over to the tank and windmill in the middle of the pasture to drink. The dog also made another trip down to the ranch buildings to see if he could pick up something more to eat, but the dogs there were watching and came swarming out with their ears flying and their tails straight up. So after plaguing them from a safe distance he went back to the pony.

After dark he slipped down the hill again and watched the dooryard until he saw the man come to the door and call the dogs inside for the night. Then he eased on down into the yard and nosed around for any scraps they might have overlooked. All he found were a few well-chewed bones, so he gnawed on one of them for a little while, until the dogs inside heard him and set up a terrific clamor to get out. He left the bone and trotted deliberately around the dooryard leaving his mark on all their favorite posts before he drifted away into the dark. By the time the man had opened the door and let them come boiling out he was safe on his knoll, where he sat hidden in the dark, watching them go tearing around down below, angrily sniffing the messages he'd left and putting out new ones of their own. After things quieted down he trotted silently back to where the blind pony was dozing in the fence corner.

The next morning the dog saw a man ride out from the corrals and come their way. It was the rancher, who had spotted the strange horse in his pasture, coming to investigate. He rode up and looked them over from a distance, while the dog lay between the pony's forefeet and growled.

"So you're the feller that's been playin' tricks on my dogs, are you?" he said to the dog.

He rode slowly around the pony looking for a brand. But the pony was slick as a tomcat, for the boy had never gotten around to branding him. There was no way for the man to tell who his owner was. He clucked to the pony and slapped a rope end against his chaps while the dog growled and trotted along under the pony's

nose to lead him away, keeping one eye cocked
back at the rider, ready to turn back if he
crowded too close.

The rancher hazed them gently along the
fence, back through the gate they'd come in, and
along the rimrock a mile or so around an angle of
the drift fence, where he left them. As he rode
back, he fastened the gate behind him.

Wolf Trap

A few days later they were down in a flat valley where there were some springs and a few cottonwood trees. The grass was good and for several days the pony seemed content to stay there. When the dog would get restless and trot off in the general direction of the rimrock and the fence, the pony, instead of following as he usually did, would throw up his head and listen to the padding of the dog's feet but make no other move. When the dog would turn his head and whine the pony might follow for a little way but soon he'd stop or begin grazing back toward the trees.

The dog fussed and worried, for he was getting mighty hungry, besides being lonely for the ranch, the boy, and the old cowboy. The first day he had found some field mice in the remains of an old hay stack, but the ones that were left were now much too careful for him to catch.

The dog was getting more and more restless, when one moonlight night they heard the howling of gray wolves on the prowl. It was a little too early for the old ones to be teaching the pups to hunt, but neither the dog nor the pony wanted to meet even a lone gray hunting by himself. They paced around nervously, constantly sniffing the wind for any sign of the wolves, and the pony stamped and snorted at every small sound.

The moon was almost down and the patches of shadow had grown long and dark when they heard something scrambling around in the buckbrush behind them and smelled an unfamiliar strong animal smell. It might have been a late-moving badger or skunk, but the pony was panic-stricken and whirled, snorting, to run without waiting for the dog. The ground was level and he was running fast with no thought of what might be in his way. In plain sight in the moonlight was part of an old stockyard fence — kinked and rusty barbed wire and a few broken posts. The dog saw it and was hurrying to lead the pony around but couldn't get there in time.

A loop of the rusty wire tightened around the blind pony's front feet, throwing him with a crash that jarred the breath out of him. Luckily, when he fell, the loosened wire dropped away from him and he was free again without being badly hurt. However, he was very frightened and shaken as well as cut a little around his front feet. He lay on the ground, shivering and getting his breath back in great sobs, while the dog trotted anxiously around him, whining, sniffing him over and licking his muzzle and face.

After a while the pony got to his feet and stood with his legs braced, breathing hard and trembling. When the dog whined for him to follow and started to trot away he wouldn't move a step at first, but snorted and whinnied for the dog to come back. When he did finally move away he snuffed and tested the ground ahead before each step for the first hundred yards or so. Even after they were moving steadily over the flat away from there and had a good solid path underfoot, he followed so closely he was nearly trampling the dog's heels at every step.

In the morning they were still traveling and soon after sun-up came in sight of a sheep herder's canvas-covered wagon. The herder and the dogs were already out on the grazing ground with the sheep so the wagon was deserted. The dog found a few scraps of cornbread and meat the herder's dogs had overlooked and licked out some tin cans that had once held beans.

In the afternoon they came on another trail leading up to the rimrock, and it was while going up that trail that the dog nearly came to grief. He'd left the pony grazing on a little bench while he trotted off to see about a dried-up cow's carcass he smelled on the wind. The sun and wind had dried it nearly as hard as flint, making it useless for food, but nonetheless the dog examined it carefully. He saw where magpies and coyotes had worked on it months before, hollowing out the inside until only a shell was left, and a badger had burrowed under it at a later time. He sniffed all around it, learning what he could of the ani-

mals that had been there ahead of him, leaving word of his own visit for others to read. He had just finished and was kicking in the grass, getting ready to leave, when a coyote trap, long buried and forgotten by the trapper who'd set it, snapped on a hind foot.

He yelped and jumped but the chain brought him up short. Luckily the trap had been so long buried that the jaws were clogged with grass and trash which kept them from snapping tight enough to break any bones. As soon as the chain stopped him the dog turned to fight the thing dragging on his foot. The heavy trap clanked and the chain rattled as he snapped and bit at it. He soon saw that it wasn't a live thing he was fighting, so after he'd sniffed the trap all over and licked his trapped foot he tried pulling loose again. If the chain had been fastened to a stake or something solid he could have pulled his foot out. For that very reason the old trappers fastened their traps to clogs of wood instead. So when the dog pulled against the trap the heavy clog dragged after him. He could drag such a weight only a few feet at a time.

After he'd fought the thing a while he started back to the colt. He'd drag the clog and trap along a little, then stop to rest and lick his foot and gnaw at the trap. The moon was up and the bull bats were booming in the dark before he was close enough to the pony to hear him whinnying for him.

As the dog scrambled down a cut-bank the clog tumbled down the bank past him, catching the chain around the roots of a bush so it jammed. The dog was jerked to a sudden stop. With the chain anchored he braced himself and pulled against the trap. After a few minutes' struggle his foot slid out of the rusty jaws, leaving him free.

His foot hurt and his leg felt sprained as he limped the rest of the way back to where the colt waited for him. He lay down and licked his foot while the pony nosed him all over, nickering softly. The dog had lost some skin on his leg where the trap had rubbed him, and on his toes as they pulled out from between the iron jaws. He wasn't hurt otherwise, although every muscle in his body would be sore for some time.

When he had rested a while he led the pony

back to the trail. They went away from there, traveling slowly but not stopping again until they had come out on top of the rimrock and up against the fence again.

They dawdled along the next few days, the dog favoring his sore leg and both of them enjoying the cool weather that had come. There was no moon now so they didn't travel at night. After the trouble they'd had they didn't stay in any one place long. Most of the time they drifted along the fence, but when they did go down into the badlands for water, they drank and rested, then moved restlessly on.

The pony's coat was a little muddy and his mane and tail were full of burrs. Except for that and the half-healed scars from his trouble with the mustangs and the barbed wire he looked about as he had when the horse thieves had turned him loose, for the grass had been good and he'd lost no weight. But the dog's ribs were showing through his hide and his long hair was matted with burrs and mud. His feet hurt him and he still limped from where he'd strained his leg in the coyote trap. Altogether he was showing considerable wear and tear. Nonetheless he still trotted alertly ahead of the pony, picking out paths for him.

Prairie Fire

One morning when the dog got up from his bed in the grass to stretch and scratch, he noticed a strange yellowish haze hanging over the badlands, and a faint acrid smell in the air. The pony noticed it too, for he stood sniffing the still air in all directions and stamping nervously.

A big prairie fire was burning somewhere, but with no wind blowing the faint trace of smoke spread the same in all directions and it was impossible to tell where it came from.

The fear of fire is strong in animals, so during the day, as the haze and the smell of smoke grew stronger, the dog and the blind pony often stood for long minutes sniffing the air, trying to locate the direction of the danger.

All over the badlands, animals and birds were uneasy. The jack rabbits came out of their bed places early and moved around nervously, often stopping to stand still and straight on their hind legs while they tested the air in all directions with their long ears and sensitive, wriggling noses. The sage chickens moved in close groups, clucking fretfully. The little birds, even the meadow larks, were quiet. When they did move, they flew close to the ground and only for short distances.

The next morning the smoke was thicker, irritating the animals' noses and eyes. The sun looked red and gave a yellow light that cast no shadows. The dog whined and led the pony little distances this way and that, but the smoke was the same everywhere so he was unable to make up his mind which way to go. The pony grazed a little, but mostly he followed close on the dog's heels with his muzzle almost in the dog's shaggy fur.

In the afternoon heavier streaks of smoke began to drift past them like mist, and behind them the dog saw other dark clouds of smoke, dun colored and dark brown, boil up into the sky from time to time. Herds of cattle and an occasional band of range horses began to drift toward them, away from the fire. Now the dog knew which way to go.

He and the pony could hear the uneasy bawling of the cattle, and their own fear grew stronger. Before long they, too, started moving away from the direction of the fire.

Out across the flats the dog saw more and more cattle and horses traveling ahead of the smoke, and other long lines of them drifting down the trails from the ridges. Once he saw a band of antelope passing, almost invisible with their light tan coats in the yellow haze.

When night came they were so uncomfortable from the bitter smoke that they kept moving, and on all sides they could hear other animals moving in the dark. Around the water holes horses squealed and kicked and cattle bawled and rattled their horns as strange herds crowded in on one another to drink.

The dog was doing his best to keep clear of the moving masses of animals. Time after time he had to lead the pony in wide circles when he heard the clicking and creaking sounds of cattle or the solider thudding sounds of moving horses overtaking them. As they came out on high ground now and again, crossing the ridges, the dog could see behind him, miles away, the long lines of tiny flickering lights that made up the broad front of the fire.

By daylight they had worked themselves out of the path of the moving herds, and found water in some small seeps in a side canyon. A coyote came padding out of the smoke and drank close by, lapping the water thirstily, and paid no attention to either the dog and pony or the sage chickens and other birds that flew in silently to drink. The coyote drank quickly, licked the water off his chops and trotted on up the canyon. A big jack rabbit hurrying jerkily down the trail passed within a few feet of him without either noticing the other.

The smoke was much thicker than it had been the day before, and small cinders floated down here and there. The pony was fearful and crowded close to the dog, touching him with his muzzle every now and again as if to make sure he was still there. When they had finished drinking the dog led the way up the deserted canyon. In a few hundred yards the trail petered out and the canyon ended in a blank wall. After whining and sniffing around the base of the steep banks for a while, the dog turned and led the way back over the trail they'd just come up. By now the pony crowded him so close the dog often had to break into a trot to keep from getting his heels trampled.

When they came out on the flats again the dog could see herds of horses and cattle moving everywhere he looked. The trails were converging on Big Foot Pass where there was a way up the Great Wall and out of the badlands. As more and more of the trails came together the herds began to mix and lose their outlines.

At first many short and savage fights broke out between wild stallions when their mares were crowded from one bunch into another. But later, as the smoke got thicker and the hot wind began dropping still glowing embers to sting their hides, they all lost interest in everything but moving ahead, away from the smoke and heat. The dog forgot his fear of the range cattle, and, except for an odd cow making a short run at him if they happened to come face to face, they paid no attention to him.

Nearer the Pass the flats were covered with

84

milling, bawling cattle, and horses flung their heads and snorted and whinnied. Rabbits, and now and then a coyote with his brush low, ran round and about under the hoofs of the bigger animals. Antelope, singly and in small bunches, mixed with the other stock.

A solid line of mixed stock moved steadily up the paths leading through the Pass.

The pony whinnied and snorted, clearing his nostrils and stamping uneasily, confused and frightened as much by movement and noise as by the smoke. He followed the dog through the little open spaces that appeared and disappeared like channels in drifting ice, as the range stock milled around. The closer they came to the Pass the tighter the animals were packed until the open spaces were no longer to be found. So the dog began working his way around the fringes of the herds, not wanting to lead the pony into the crush where they might get separated or hurt.

As more and more herds came from the direction of the fire, both cattle and horses were forced up into the nearby canyons by the crowding, and before long the dog and the pony found them-

85

selves in one of these. As the pressure from behind grew, horses began trying to climb out, rearing and plunging to get a foothold on the steep bank. After a time the bank became cut and gouged until at last one horse managed to find footing and lunge over the top of the steepest part. From there to the rimrock it was steep but the horse managed to pick a way up and was soon out on top. Other horses followed, some making it and others losing their footing and rolling back down. But it wasn't long before a rough trail had been cut out, and more and more horses had climbed to the top. Crowded from behind, the dog led the pony up the steep way, and soon came over the rimrock with the rest.

They found themselves several miles from where the trails through the Pass came out, and before they had traveled far their way was blocked again by the drift fence they had been following so long. The horses crowded along it, but one way led back toward the smoke, and the other to an apron fence or wing, that blocked all travel along the rimrock.

More and more horses crowded near the fence,

whinnying and quarreling, but not pushing the wire. After a time, the new trail up the rimrock was worn to an easier grade, and cattle began coming up, too. Unlike horses, cattle have little fear of wire, so they crowded against the fence that blocked their way.

They pushed their heads through between the strands and leaned their weight against the wires. And as more and more cattle came up the pressure on the fence increased. The wires screeched as they pulled through the staples; an occasional fence post gave way with a sharp crack. The cattle kept on crowding up while the horses milled around a little distance off, and soon wires twanged as they broke and the cattle poured through the break. Some went through draped in long loops of barbwire, but unconcernedly shook or kicked themselves loose and went on. For a while a solid mass of cattle moved over the broken fence, then as they thinned a little the horses started crossing. The dog waited until most of them were across, then he led the pony through the middle of the break, where the wire had been dragged away or trampled into the ground.

Once through the fence they were in open grass country. They drifted ahead with no obstacles to hold them back, and room enough to avoid the scattered bunches of horses and cattle that had begun to slow down and spread out when they got where the smoke was thinner and the fire brands had stopped falling.

During the night the wind changed, blowing the smoke away from them. Next morning they threaded their way between the slowly grazing herds in the general direction of the ranch.

During the day they came to fenced country again, but before long they got on a state road that ran between fences, with no gates across it. Small bunches of horses and cattle were drifting along, grazing on the grass along the sides of the road. The dog and the pony followed them, and for the first time in weeks found themselves moving steadily toward home with no fence to block their way.

Home Ranch

Back at the ranch the old cowpuncher and the boy had been watching the smoke anxiously for some days, wondering if the fire was going to spread to their part of the range. Smoke drifted low over the hills, making the sunlight yellow and strange looking. When a fire gets started on a long front a change of wind may move it in any direction. If it came their way they would help the cowboys and homesteaders fighting it, but now they were busy plowing fireguards.

First they plowed a wide strip around the ranch buildings, and after that they plowed other strips around the big fenced pastures. These strips would bar the advance of a grass fire as levees do a flooding river. In case it seemed necessary they could set backfires along the edge of the plowing, which would burn upwind to meet the advancing flame and starve it out.

After the fireguards were plowed they loaded barrels of water in the wagon, along with shovels and gunny sacks and old tarpaulins, to have them ready in case they should have to fight fire. After that they went about their business as usual.

One afternoon they were sitting on the little platform on top of the windmill tower where they had been greasing the gears. As they rested a little before climbing back down, they looked out over the big pastures where small bunches of strange horses were moving around. For a couple of days strange stock had been drifting along the road and hanging over the fence where they smelled the water in the big earth dam. The old cowpuncher knew they had been driven off their own range by the fire and that soon men would come looking for them, so he'd opened the gates and let them into the pasture.

The man and the boy sat up there enjoying the high viewpoint, watching the strange horses grazing restlessly in small, changing bunches, uneasy at being mixed up with so many strangers.

After a bit the boy suddenly spoke up. "Look

there!" he exclaimed. "Isn't that a dog with that lone horse out there?"

The old cowboy looked where the boy pointed. "Looks kinda like it," he agreed after a little. "But it's a mite hard to tell from here."

As they watched, the lone horse drifted steadily toward them, and before long they could plainly make out the dog trotting ahead, just under the horse's nose. When he was sure of this, the boy jumped up, paying no attention to the long drop below him.

"It's my blind pony and the dog!" he told the man excitedly as he scrambled for the ladder. "The dog's bringing him home!"

"Sure does look it," the old cowboy agreed as he carefully made his way over to the top of the ladder. "We'll know in a minute. But let's not break our necks on the way down."

In a few minutes the horse and dog came up on top of the hogback that hid most of the pasture from anyone standing on the ground, and the dog led the way down the trail past the washouts, across the gulch, and up to the gate of the little horse pasture. The boy ran to open the gate, touching the ground only now and again on the way, for he saw that it was surely his dog and his spotted pony.

"Well, it's them, all right," the old cowboy said as he walked up.

But the boy couldn't answer right then. He was having his hands full with the dog, who was acting like he was locoed — jumping up to lick the boy's face one minute and running around in crazy circles the next. In a few minutes he quieted down a little so the boy could get clear of him and start petting and talking to the blind pony.

"Looks like they come a right far ways," the old cowboy said. "Lookit the mud and burrs in their hair. An' the dog is a rack of bones, and footsore to boot. First thing you'd better do is feed him."

"Yessir, that's just what I'd better do!" the boy agreed.

He hurried to the house for a big plate of scraps, and the old cowboy got some grain and poured it on the ground for the pony. While

the dog gulped his feed, the boy fussed around. He'd rub the pony down for a little, and pull a few burrs out of his mane, then he'd pat the dog and try to pull loose some of his matted fur before he went back to the pony.

"Now, let's fix up that dog's feet," the cowboy suggested, coming out of the stable with lard and axle grease, some clean rags and the sheep shears.

For a long time they worked on the dog, gently cutting big mats of burrs out of his fur with the shears, and digging the festered thorns out of his feet and doctoring the places with turpentine. They cleaned out the cut places in his pads and worked lard into them and then smeared axle grease on top of that. The dog seemed to enjoy the attention he was getting, for he lay quiet and panted happily, only whining and squirming a little bit when they dug deep after the broken point of a cactus thorn or when the turpentine smarted in a cut.

When they finished with him he sat around and watched them curry the pony and trim out his mane and tail. His hoofs had grown out long

and had broken off in ragged edges, so they trimmed them up with the hoof pinchers and the rasp until they looked neat again.

"Wonder where they've been," the boy said as they doctored the cuts and burns on the pony's hide. "The dog's leg looks like he's been in a trap, and the pony has these cuts and scabs on his back and some wire cuts on his legs, besides some little burned places on both him and the dog."

"Hard to tell," the old cowboy told him as he rubbed sulphur and lard on a cut. "The horse thieves probably found out he was blind and turned him loose somewhere, and they been all this time getting back."

"But how in the world did the dog live, and how did he eat, with nobody to feed him all that time?" the boy wanted to know.

"He probably turned half coyote," the old man figured. "Sometimes a dog will do that when he's put on his own. But I reckon we'll never know for sure."

When the man and the boy had finished and were leaning on the gate a minute before they went to get their supper, the dog smelled all round the colt, touched noses with him, and sniffed his feet until he satisfied himself everything necessary had been done. Then, while the pony leaned his head over the gate and whinnied softly after him, the dog trotted off to inspect the corrals and ranch buildings, sniffing at all the familiar posts and corners to make sure things were still as he'd left them, and leaving his sign for all who might come by, so they'd know that he was back and taking care of things again.